WEEKLY READER CHILDREN'S BOOK CLUB PRESENTS

ARTHUR
and
THE GOLDEN GUINEA

STORY *and* PICTURES
by
JEAN BERWICK

GOLDEN GATE JUNIOR BOOKS

SAN CARLOS, CALIFORNIA

To Tom and Blair and Sherry

The verse on page sixteen was written by Rutherfoord Goodwin for Colonial Williamsburg.

ONCE upon a time,
when great-great-great-great-Great-
GREAT-grandfathers were little boys,
one of them was a boy named Arthur.
Arthur lived in Williamsburg,
a town in Virginia,
which was named after
King William of England.

Arthur was not a large boy
and he was not a small boy.
He was not plump or thin or tall.
He was a plain middle-sized boy,
that's all.

But something made Arthur feel very different
from the other middle-sized boys
in Williamsburg.
He carried a secret in his pocket.
In Arthur's pocket
was a beautiful round golden guinea—
a coin of pure gold. *Pure gold.*

And it was all his own.

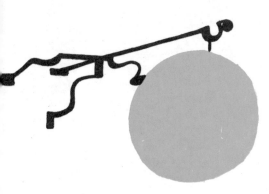

Nobody
had given Arthur
the secret gold coin
and nobody
in Williamsburg
knew that he had it.

Not the silversmith who made and mended his mother's spoons and earrings
Not the apothecary who fixed medicines for Arthur when he was sick
and sold him hard candies from a tall jar

Not the wig maker with his great powdered wigs
Not the shoemaker or the cabinetmaker or the lady who made hats.

Arthur had found the golden guinea
in a secret garden place he knew.
He often went there to dig for buried treasure.
If Arthur's mother had known about the guinea
she would have said,
"Money's to spend and money's to lend
and only a miser does hide it."
And she might have sent him to spend the coin
on a fat flat flounder at the fishmonger's,
or on some long yellow loaves of bread
from the bake shop.

Flat flounders are fine,
thought Arthur,
but not in place
of my shiny coin.
Every day
he looked at his treasure
in the sunshine.
And every night
he watched it reflect
the light of the candle
in his room.

One warm spring day Arthur's mother asked him to go
on a special errand for her. She gave him a broken silver
spoon to be repaired by Master John, the silversmith.
Arthur set out on his way.
When he came to the miller's windmill,
he could not pass by
without a ride on it—
but only for a moment.

On he went until he heard the blacksmith singing loudly
to the clang, clang, clang of his hammer.

The Smith must strike
whilst iron's hot,
And know which is,
and what is not!

Arthur watched from the doorway until he remembered
he had a special job to do.

On he went again, not even climbing up to gaze
at the candies in the window of the apothecary shop.

At the silversmith's
he handed his mother's
broken spoon
to Master John.
But when his hand
went back into his pocket
the coin was not there.
His beautiful golden guinea
was gone!

Arthur ran to the door of the shop
and looked up and down the street.
Nothing glittered, nothing shone!
He stood very still
and wondered what to do.
He felt lonely and sad.
The lady who made hats hurried past
with an armful of bows and feathers
and her nose in the air.
She didn't even see Arthur.
The wig maker walked quickly
down the wide street
on his way to the Governor's palace.
The shoemaker passed by
with a pair of new shoes.
Arthur wished he could tell someone
about his lost coin.
But nobody knew about it
and nobody cared
and nobody
noticed
him.

Suddenly there was a great rumble and a lot of dust
as the Governor's coach came rolling proudly down the street.
The Governor was dressed in his finest clothes.
Every one turned to stare at him.

The lady who made hats stared so hard that
she walked right into a mulberry tree! Bows and feathers
went flying every which way.
The wig maker shook a feather off his head and hurried on.
The shoemaker brushed a feather off the new shoes
he was carrying and walked into the apothecary shop.
The apothecary looked out of his shop window
and laughed as he sang,
Come on, Mistress High-hat,
And just follow me.
We'll try to jump over
That mulberry tree.

Master John helped the hat lady pick up bows
in front of his shop.
Arthur started to chase the feathers here and there
and everywhere.
The men on the sidewalk laughed and laughed
until Arthur felt very silly. But he too had lost something
that day and he wanted to help the lady.

At last he had caught
all the feathers but one.
It was a round fluffy feather.
It floated up and down
and around
and around
all the way to the miller's windmill
before it came to rest.

Gently Arthur picked it up.
And at that moment he saw something
gleam and glitter in the dust under
the windmill. It was something round
and gold and beautiful.
It was his own wonderful guinea!
Arthur started to put the coin back
in his pocket, but suddenly he knew he
couldn't keep it a secret for another moment.
He had to tell *everyone!*
"Look! Look what I found," he shouted.
"I found it one day in my secret garden place.
This morning I lost it and now
I've found it again."

Everyone looked at
the golden coin.
Everyone agreed
that Arthur
was the most fortunate
boy in all Williamsburg.
And Arthur's mother
did not say,
"Money's to spend
and money's to lend."
She told Arthur
that he must keep
the golden guinea
always
            for good luck.
            And he did.